ESCAPE FROM THE FIERCE PREDATOR

Other books in the series:

Attack of the
LIZARD KING

Charge of the
THREE-HORNED MONSTER

March of the
ARMOURED BEASTS

Flight of the
WINGED SERPENT

Catching the
SPEEDY THIEF

Stampede of the
GIANT REPTILES

Rescuing the
PLATED LIZARD

Swimming with the
SEA MONSTER

Tracking the
GIGANTIC BEAST

DINOSAUR COVE™

ESCAPE FROM THE FIERCE PREDATOR

by
REX STONE

illustrated by
MIKE SPOOR

Series created by
Working Partners Ltd

OXFORD
UNIVERSITY PRESS

Special thanks to Jan Burchett and Sara Vogler

For Claire Heywood, Nick Teare and Kevin Dawson from
Auntie Sara! – R.S.

These illustrations are for Daniel and Thomas Ogles, and all
the children at St.Katherine's CE Primary School – M.S.

OXFORD
UNIVERSITY PRESS

Great Clarendon Street, Oxford OX2 6DP
Oxford University Press is a department of the University of Oxford.
It furthers the University's objective of excellence in research, scholarship,
and education by publishing worldwide in

Oxford   New York

Auckland   Cape Town   Dar es Salaam   Hong Kong   Karachi
Kuala Lumpur   Madrid   Melbourne   Mexico City   Nairobi
New Delhi   Shanghai   Taipei   Toronto

With offices in

Argentina   Austria   Brazil   Chile   Czech Republic   France   Greece
Guatemala   Hungary   Italy   Japan   Poland   Portugal   Singapore
South Korea   Switzerland   Thailand   Turkey   Ukraine   Vietnam

Oxford is a registered trade mark of Oxford University Press
in the UK and in certain other countries

British Library Cataloguing in Publication Data

Data available

ISBN: 978-0-19-272895-1

1 3 5 7 9 10 8 6 4 2

Printed in Great Britain by CPI Cox and Wyman, Reading, Berkshire
Paper used in the production of this book is a natural,
recyclable product made from wood grown in sustainable forests
The manufacturing process conforms to the environmental
regulations of the country of origin

FACT FILE

➡ JAMIE HAS JUST MOVED FROM THE CITY TO LIVE IN THE LIGHTHOUSE IN DINOSAUR COVE. JAMIE'S DAD IS OPENING A DINOSAUR MUSEUM ON THE BOTTOM FLOOR OF THE LIGHTHOUSE. WHEN JAMIE GOES HUNTING FOR FOSSILS IN THE CRUMBLING CLIFFS ON THE BEACH HE MEETS A LOCAL BOY, TOM, AND THE TWO DISCOVER AN AMAZING SECRET: A WORLD WITH REAL, LIVE DINOSAURS! DINOSAURS USE THEIR SENSE OF SMELL TO HELP THEM HUNT, SO THE BOYS HAVE TO MAKE SURE THEY STAY DOWNWIND!

JAMIE

- **FULL NAME:** JAMIE MORGAN
- **AGE:** 8 YEARS
- **SIZE:** 1 JATOM*
- **TOP SPEED:** 10 KPH
- **LIKES:** FOSSIL HUNTING AND LEARNING ABOUT DINOSAURS
- **DISLIKES:** BEING STUCK INDOORS

Jamie's eye

Jamie's foot

Jamie's hand

*NOTE: A JATOM IS THE SIZE OF JAMIE OR TOM: 125 CM TALL AND 27 KG IN WEIGHT

TOM

- **FULL NAME:** THOMAS CLAY
- **AGE:** 8 YEARS
- **SIZE:** 1 JATOM*
- **TOP SPEED:** 10 KPH
- **LIKES:** TRACKING ANIMALS AND EXPLORING WILDLIFE
- **DISLIKES:** RAINY DAYS

Tom's eye

Tom's hand

WANNA

- **FULL NAME:** WANNANOSAURUS
- **AGE:** 65 – 80 MILLION YEARS**
- **SIZE:** LESS THAN A JATOM*
- **TOP SPEED:** 50 KPH, ESPECIALLY WHEN BEING CHASED BY A T-REX
- **LIKES:** STINKY GINGKO FRUIT AND BANGING HIS HEAD ON TREE TRUNKS
- **DISLIKES:** SCARY DINOSAURS

Wanna's head

Wanna's foot

*NOTE: A JATOM IS THE SIZE OF JANIE OR TOM: 125 CM TALL AND 27 KG IN WEIGHT
**NOTE: SCIENTISTS CALL THIS PERIOD THE LATE CRETACEOUS

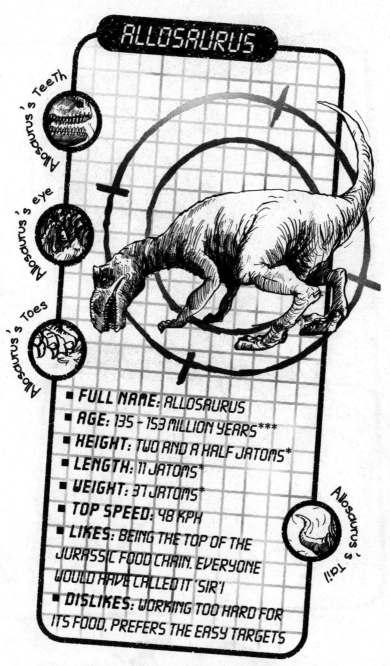

ALLOSAURUS

Allosaurus's Teeth

Allosaurus's eye

Allosaurus's Toes

Allosaurus's Tail

- **FULL NAME:** ALLOSAURUS
- **AGE:** 135 - 153 MILLION YEARS***
- **HEIGHT:** TWO AND A HALF JATOMS*
- **LENGTH:** 11 JATOMS*
- **WEIGHT:** 37 JATOMS*
- **TOP SPEED:** 48 KPH
- **LIKES:** BEING THE TOP OF THE JURASSIC FOOD CHAIN. EVERYONE WOULD HAVE CALLED IT 'SIR'!
- **DISLIKES:** WORKING TOO HARD FOR ITS FOOD. PREFERS THE EASY TARGETS

*NOTE: A JATOM IS THE SIZE OF JAMIE OR TOM: 125 CM TALL AND 27 KG IN WEIGHT
***NOTE: SCIENTISTS CALL THIS PERIOD THE JURASSIC

DINOSAUR COVE

Village

Marina

SealighT Head

Landslips where clay and fossils are

Muddy beach

DINO CAVE

High Tide beach line

Low Tide beach line

Sea

Smuggler's Point

'Quiet please, everybody,' Jamie Morgan called, waving his arms to get the attention of his dino-mad audience.

Jamie's best friend Tom Clay cleared his throat and used his best TV presenter voice. 'The great dinosaur quiz is about to begin.'

Jamie's dad handed out the last clipboard and pencil to the crowd of eager children and gave Jamie and Tom high fives. 'Thanks for your help, guys,' he said. 'I can take it from here.'

'I wish we could join in,' whispered Tom, as they stepped away.

'It wouldn't be fair,' Jamie reminded him. 'Dad said we're such dino experts we'd be bound to win.'

Tom nudged Jamie. 'He has no idea!'

The boys had discovered an entrance to a secret world of living dinosaurs. It was hidden deep in the cliff, inside an old smugglers' cave, and they visited it as often as they could.

Jamie's dad read the first question, taken from a talk he'd given earlier that day. 'Which dinosaur was one of the biggest Jurassic predators and had a name that means "different lizard"?'

There was a noisy
tapping of pencils as
everyone wrote the
answer down.

'Easy,' murmured Jamie. 'Allosaurus.'

After a couple more easy questions, Jamie's
dad said, 'Now you'll have to put on your
thinking caps. What newly discovered
dinosaur from the Cretaceous period
had slender arms and long bones in the
hand with claws that look like sickles?
It was probably covered in feathers.'

'That's hard!' whispered Jamie, trying
to remember. 'I think it's a therizinosaurid.'

Tom nodded in agreement. It didn't look
as though many people were writing down an
answer. 'Newly discovered dinosaurs are tricky.'

Jamie's eyes lit up. 'I've just had an idea!
What if *we* discovered a dinosaur that *no one*
knew about?'

'And I know just where we could do that . . . ' said Tom.

Jamie knew what Tom was thinking. 'Dino World here we come!'

Jamie grabbed his backpack and waved to his dad. The boys sprinted out of the lighthouse towards their secret world.

'Off on another adventure?' Jamie's grandad called as the boys passed him fishing on the beach.

'You bet!' Jamie replied.

Soon the boys were in their secret cave and Jamie flashed his torch over the fossilized footprints on the floor.

'Here we go!' he said, placing his feet in the footprints. Tom followed close behind. In an instant they were in the hot Jurassic sunshine of their amazing secret world.

Grunk!

A little green and brown dinosaur bounded up.

'We're back, Wanna,' cried Jamie as their prehistoric friend gave them a nudge with his hard, bony head.

The wannanosaurus wagged his tail in excitement.

Tom looked around the cycads and conifers of the steamy jungle. 'Where would be the best place to find an undiscovered dino?'

'Let's climb that tree and look around,' suggested Jamie.

The conifer branches were well spaced and the fern-like leaves easily pushed out of the way. Tom and Jamie climbed the tree like a ladder.

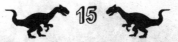

Grunk?

A puzzled Wanna watched
them from far below as the boys scaled
the tree almost to the very top.

'Awesome!' said Tom, looking
through his binoculars. He turned
an excited face to Jamie. 'You won't
believe what I've just seen.'

Tom handed Jamie his binoculars
and Jamie followed Tom's
directions.

'Allosaurs!' Jamie
gasped. 'A whole herd.'
Out on the open plains, he spotted
a group of fierce-looking dinosaurs
with big heads and long, thick tails.

'It's not an undiscovered
dinosaur,' Tom said. 'But we've
never seen one before.'

Jamie kept watch through the binoculars. 'Are they asleep? They're not moving much.'

'A rare find, indeed,' said Tom in his wildlife presenter voice, peering into an imaginary camera. 'Not just one allosaurus—the king of the Jurassic beasts—but . . . ' He squinted and tried to count. 'Twenty of the elusive dinosaurs. What could these ferocious creatures be up to?'

'There's only one way to find out,' Jamie piped up. 'We've got to get a closer look.'

CHAPTER 2

The boys climbed down the tree to an excited Wanna. Tom collected several gingko fruits from nearby and stuffed them into Jamie's backpack. 'In case we need to keep Wanna quiet.'

They hurried through the thick undergrowth, heading westwards for the plains and the allosaurs. At the edge of the jungle, Tom pointed to a small outcrop of rocks about the length of a swimming pool from the herd and not too far from the tree line.

'We can hide behind those rocks and observe,' said Tom. 'But watch for any signs of allosaur movement.'

The boys crept over the dry plains with Wanna at their heels and crouched behind a large rock. Wanna hunkered down next to them.

'What a great view!' whispered Jamie. He peered round the rock and studied the sleeping allosaurs. The beasts surrounded a huge dinosaur carcass. 'Dinner time's over, I reckon.'

'Now they're having a nap,' Tom added, pretending to snap a photo with an imaginary camera. The allosaurs were hunched down, squatting on their powerful back legs. Their heads were bent forward on their chests. Dino bones, nearly picked clean, were scattered among the sleeping beasts.

Jamie pulled out his Fossil Finder and typed in '*ALLOSAURUS*'.

'*THE LARGEST CARNIVORE OF THE JURASSIC PERIOD, UP TO TWELVE METRES IN LENGTH,*' he read. '*LONG CLAWS ON THREE-FINGERED HANDS, AND LARGE, POWERFUL JAWS. HUNTED IN PACKS AND HAD A GOOD SENSE OF SMELL.*' Jamie looked up at the carnivores. 'Uh oh. What if they smell us?'

'The wind is coming from the north,' said Tom, holding a wet finger in the air. 'Unless the wind changes, they won't be able to smell us.'

A pterosaur screeched overhead and disturbed two of the smaller allosaurs, who woke up and began to nudge each other playfully.

'The adults are taking a well-earned rest after a successful hunt,' said Tom into an imaginary microphone. 'The youngsters have other ideas. Their bellies may be full, but they're not going to waste time snoozing.'

One of the young allosaurs knocked the other into an adult allosaurus, waking it up. The largest allosaurus got to its feet and gave a roar.

'Nap's over,' Jamie said nervously, hoping the wind wasn't going to change. He didn't want any of those allosaurs to come looking for a tasty boy-sized pudding.

Most of the group woke up, shook their heads and stamped their feet, crushing the remains of their dinner. Jamie held his breath.

The allosaurs began moving across the plains away from the rocky outcrop, and Jamie exhaled. Soon, all the allosaurs had stalked off, except for one still dozing in the sun.

Wanna began to fidget.

'Sorry, boy,' said Jamie. 'We're not ready to go just yet. There's still one allie that's not leaving.'

'It's still asleep,' Tom said. 'See its front legs twitching. Like a dog when it dreams.'

25

Wanna stood up and
began to nudge the boys. 'Wanna
thinks it's playtime,' Jamie said, scratching
Wanna under his chin. 'Why don't you give
him a few gingkoes to keep him quiet?'

Tom rummaged in Jamie's backpack for a
gingko. As soon as Tom held up the round,
ripe gingko, Wanna lunged for it, knocking it

out of Tom's hand. Tom and Jamie watched in horror as the gingko rolled across the ground stopping just in front of the sleeping allie.

Before the boys could stop him, Wanna darted after his favourite snack right up to the allosaurus. If the allosaurus woke up, Wanna would be its after-dinner treat!

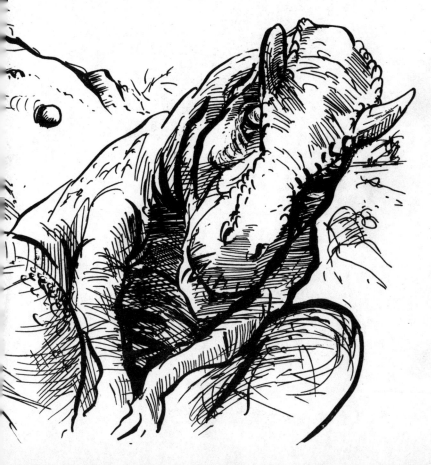

The boys whispered furiously at Wanna to come back, but the little dino was too focused on searching for his snack.

Tom waved another gingko at him but they couldn't get Wanna's attention.

'We've got to go and get him,' Jamie said.

Tom groaned and the boys crept out from behind the rock, closer and closer, until they could almost touch the bulky body of the sleeping beast. Its mouth was slightly open and they could just see the long, sharp teeth.

'Listen to it snore!' whispered Jamie.

'Look at those claws,' said Tom.
'They're as long as my hand.'

Just then, the allosaurus snorted in its
sleep, making the boys jump.

'Let's get Wanna and get out of here,'
Jamie decided.

The boys grabbed Wanna, who had
just found the gingko, and pulled
him to the safety of a clump of
ferns nearer to the jungle.

'That's as close as I ever want
to get to an allosaurus,' Tom said.

'It was pretty amazing,' Jamie said, glancing
back to make sure the allie was still asleep.

Each boy grabbed one of Wanna's front paws
and began to walk towards the thick jungle.
The air was suddenly full of a hideous stink.

'Phwoa!' Tom gasped. 'What's that horrible
smell? It's worse than a gingko fruit.'

'Wasn't me.' Jamie laughed and then
spotted several brown, steaming mounds nearly
as tall as he was just ahead. 'Allosaurus poo!'

'Gross.' Tom grinned. 'You'd need a huge
pooper-scooper for that lot.'

'And a million cans of air freshener!' Jamie
chuckled. 'Why didn't we smell this before?'

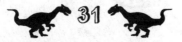

'The wind must have changed,' Tom
said. He paused, realizing what he had
just said.

'If we can smell the poo, then that
means that . . . ' Jamie started.

'The allie can smell us,' Tom finished.

The boys and Wanna turned round just
in time to see the huge, sleepy allosaurus
open one eye.

The allosaurus lifted its head and
sniffed the air.

'Uh oh,' whispered
Tom. The
boys and
Wanna backed
away quickly.

The great beast
moved its head
slowly from side
to side.

'It's trying to work out the strange new smell,' said Jamie. 'It won't be long before it decides we're pudding.'

'Let's get to the trees!' Tom shouted.

The allosaurus raised itself off its haunches and slowly lumbered in their direction.

The boys shot off across the plains with Wanna galloping at their side.

'It's still sleepy,' shouted Tom, glancing back. 'Maybe we can outrun it.'

But before the boys could get to the tree line, the allosaurus swung round, cutting off their access. This was a predator who knew how to hunt.

The boys made
a speedy U-turn and
headed away from the
jungle and the allosaurus. They
could hear the allie's thumping
footsteps behind.

'Keep running,' yelled Tom.
'It's picking up speed!'

The boys and Wanna raced forward
through the now rocky terrain. The
ground began to steadily slope upwards.
It was hard to sprint—and the allosaurus was
getting closer.

Suddenly, Jamie skidded to a halt.
'Oh no!' he groaned, looking
down at the huge, deep
canyon below him.

One wrong step and
they would tumble over the
edge. There was nowhere left
to run.

'It's the massive canyon,' said
Tom in a panic. 'What are we going
to do?'

Jamie turned to see the allosaurus
bearing down on them. 'We're dead meat.'

'Look!' Tom shouted. 'There's a ledge
down there.'

Jamie saw the shelf of rock beneath them.
It was just wide enough . . .

'We've got to jump!' yelled Tom.

Grabbing Wanna, the boys took a deep breath and jumped onto the narrow ledge. All three landed safely and looked up to the edge of the canyon.

A terrifying roar sounded over their heads and

SNAP!

Sharp teeth gnashed in the air just above them. The boys and Wanna flattened themselves on the ledge. They could feel the allie's hot breath on the back of their necks.

The allie roared in fury and stamped its feet, sending down a shower of rocks and dust. It couldn't lean over far enough to reach them.

'It's having a tantrum because its pudding has escaped.' Tom gave a wobbly grin.

With each pounding step above them, more earth and stones from the walls of the canyon rained down on them.

CRACK!

A fissure appeared in the rock they were lying on.

'What if the ledge breaks from all that stomping?' hissed Tom.

'Then we're in even bigger trouble,' Jamie replied.

Wanna cowered against the tumbling rocks and backed along the ledge, grunking in terror.

Another loud crack sounded—the ledge was splitting away from the wall!

41

When Jamie looked back, Wanna
had disappeared.

Tom and Jamie crawled along the
cracking ledge to where they last saw Wanna
and heard a distinct grunk. Jamie looked
towards the wall and saw an opening with
a pair of beady eyes staring at him.

Grunk! Grunk!

Wanna had found a small cave in the wall
of the canyon. The boys squeezed in after
him, away from the treacherous ledge. 'Well
done, Wanna,' he said. 'You've found us a
really good hiding place.'

Wanna grunked happily.

'Once the allie gets bored we can escape,'
said Tom, as they listened to the angry
stamping overhead.

But the sounds of bellowing grew louder. Wanna cowered behind Jamie.

'Don't worry, Wanna,' said Jamie. 'We're safe here.'

'I'm not so sure,' said Tom and pointed to the mouth of the cave.

Shards of rock showered down from the cave entrance as the allie's massive feet pounded above.

'It's going to collapse!' Tom shouted.

The boys and Wanna leaped back just in time.

 43

CRASH!

The rock above the cave mouth tumbled down, sending up clouds of dust. The cave was plunged into darkness.

'I can't see a thing,' whispered Tom.

Jamie felt round in his backpack for his torch and pulled it out. A huge pile of stones and rocks was blocking their exit. 'We're trapped,' he said.

'We'd need a bulldozer to shift that lot,' said Tom. 'What do we do now? We're stuck in a cave, millions of years in the past.'

Jamie shone his torch over the cave. The jagged walls stretched away into the dark. 'Maybe there's a way out this way.' Jamie took a tentative step forward.

'Let's see where it goes,' Tom said.

Bent double, Jamie led the way over the sloping, slippery floor. Jamie soon had to take off his backpack to squeeze through the narrow passage. The air became cooler as they went deeper underground.

At last the tunnel opened up and they could walk along without stooping.

'Look at these scratches!' Jamie shone his torch on the wall. 'And there's more on the floor, too.'

'Three lines together each time,' said Tom, tracing the shallow scratches with his fingers.

'They could be claw marks,' said Jamie. 'A dinosaur must have come this way.'

'One with big feet,' agreed Tom. 'Those marks are deep.'

'That's great news.' Jamie walked faster.

'Coming face-to-face with a vicious, sharp-clawed dinosaur isn't great news,' Tom said.

'It means there might be another way out of here,' said Jamie. 'The dinosaur that made these marks couldn't have squeezed through the narrow tunnel behind us. It came in from somewhere else.'

'Good thinking!' exclaimed Tom.

Wanna grunked, ran ahead and turned, his head cocked.

Jamie laughed. 'I think he wants us to hurry up!'

The boys moved along the tunnel faster, now, until it split into two passages.

'Which one do we take?' Tom wondered.

Jamie examined the two tunnels in the torchlight. 'The scratch marks go along the one on the right. If we follow them we might find the way out.'

Jamie walked down the tunnel, but Tom didn't move. 'Did you hear something?' he whispered.

Jamie shook his head. Just as he took a step forward, a short, high-pitched screech filled the air. Jamie stumbled back into Tom.

'There is definitely something in here,' Tom said.

Jamie shone his torch down the tunnel, but there was no sign of any creature. 'We'll just have to hope that we don't run into it.'

'And that we find
the exit soon,' replied Tom.
Jamie led the way, flashing his
torch all around. The shadows from the
beam made strange shapes over the craggy
walls. Tom followed with Wanna, keeping as
close as he could to the light.

Suddenly, something darted across the
beam of the torch ahead.

'What was that?' whispered Jamie in alarm,
trying to catch the creature in the light.

'I don't know!' Tom said. 'But it's
heading this way!'

SCREEE!

A dinosaur burst out of the darkness towards them. Wanna gave a frightened grunk.

But Jamie stood his ground. 'If it's used to the dark it won't like this.' He held up his torch and shone it into the dinosaur's eyes.

As the bright beam flashed down the tunnel, the boys caught a glimpse of two monstrous yellow eyes glaring at them.

The creature gave a
sharp cry and cowered
back into the shadows.
'It's working!'
exclaimed Tom.

But the
words were hardly
out of his mouth when
another ear-splitting screech
filled the air and the dinosaur was upon
them, rearing up to attack. Long, sharp claws
reached towards Jamie. He flung his arms up to
protect himself and the torch fell from his hand.

Terrified, the boys cowered back into the darkness of the tunnel; Wanna pressed close between them. They could hear the torch being banged against the cave walls and the tunnel was filled with strange flashes of light.

'It's smashing my torch!' cried Jamie.

There was a CRACK! and the tunnel was plunged into complete darkness.

'We're in big trouble,' Jamie said, trying to feel his way back along the tunnel. 'It knows its way in the dark—and we don't.'

'I think it's coming!' Tom whispered.

The boys frantically hurried down the tunnel, scraping their arms and legs. Wanna was grunking with fear.

'We're where the tunnel divides,' came Tom's voice. 'Let's go down this other one.'

'And let's hurry!' Jamie replied.

'Suppose the dino *lives* underground,' panted Tom as they stumbled blindly along. 'There might not be another way out.'

'There has to be,' said Jamie.

The new tunnel twisted and turned, and they could feel the ground sloping upwards as they scrambled to escape the dinosaur. It was catching them up and the boys could hear the hiss of its breathing.

'There's light ahead!' exclaimed Jamie.

They could dimly see the tunnel opening out into a cavern.

They ran towards it.
Through a small crack
in the high roof was—daylight!
'Our escape route!' cried Tom,
pointing to a steep path up to
the opening.

SCREEE!

The boys whirled round in fright. The dinosaur emerged from the tunnel behind them.

It was an extraordinary sight. The creature stood on two spindly legs, its feet wide and webbed. Its front legs were thin and bony; its body was covered in pale, almost transparent skin and its huge head had a beaked mouth and pointed front teeth. Two round eyes as big as digestive biscuits blinked blindly in the light.

'I've never seen anything like that,' murmured Tom in astonishment.

'Whatever it is, it's still got my torch!' exclaimed Jamie. The strange dinosaur was brandishing the broken torch in its long claws.

As its eyes got used to the light, it moved towards the boys and Wanna. The three friends inched back, never taking their eyes off it.

Jamie reached into his backpack and pulled out a gingko.

'I'll try and hold it off while you
see how we get out.'
Jamie threw the fruit
at the dinosaur
while Tom dashed
across the cavern.
The gingko hit it
square in the chest
and it leaped back with
another shriek. Jamie
threw a second one.

Grunk!

Wanna didn't like watching his gingkoes
sail away.

The mysterious dinosaur dashed towards
Jamie again just as he threw another fruit.
The gingko landed smack on the dinosaur's
face, splattering it with gingko juice.

A long, purple tongue licked the juice off
its face, and the dinosaur stopped charging.

Then it dropped
the torch on the
floor, took a squashed
gingko in its claw
and began to eat it
with great slurping
noises.

From across the
cavern and partway up the steep
path, Tom called out, 'There are footholds.
We can make it!'

Jamie watched the pale, skinny
dinosaur eating the
gingko. It didn't look
very aggressive any
more, gobbling up the
gingko fruits. Jamie took
another gingko, just in
case, and crept towards
the big-eyed dinosaur.

'What are you doing?' Tom hissed.

'Trying to get the torch back,' Jamie said slowly and calmly. 'We can't leave anything in Dino World, remember?'

He took one step, then another. He could almost reach the torch. Jamie rolled the gingko fruit to the dinosaur's feet and, while it grabbed the fruit, Jamie snatched the torch.

EEE EEE EEE!

The dinosaur was enjoying the gingkoes and didn't make a move when Jamie backed away towards Tom and the path up to the top of the cavern. It looked as if their scary dinosaur was vegetarian after all.

'Let's get out of here,' Tom said, tempting Wanna up the steep climb to the hole in the cavern roof using a gingko. He held it out to make Wanna stretch as high as he could to bite it, and Jamie pushed Wanna from behind.

Grunk!

Wanna scrambled up the steep wall of the cavern, with his favourite food just out of reach. Jamie clambered up after him and at last they were near the opening. They could see blue sky above.

'We're almost out,' Tom said.

But when Jamie looked closely, he could see that the hole was much too small, even for Wanna. 'We'll never fit through.'

'We have to,' Tom said. 'There's no other way out.'

Grunk!

Wanna took two steps back, charged forward and, with a tremendous thump, headbutted the rock.

'It's cracking,' said Jamie. 'Wanna to the rescue!'

The little dino rammed the opening again. Stones and earth fell away. Then he squeezed through and disappeared.

'Hooray!' the boys cheered.

Jamie and Tom pulled themselves through the hole. At last they were lying on their backs in the hot sunlight, with Wanna galloping round in delight.

'Clever boy.' Jamie patted Wanna on the head. 'You deserve a gingko feast.'

'Hey, we're back where we started,' said Tom. 'At the top of Massive Canyon.'

Jamie got out his Fossil Finder. 'Let's find out what that weird dino was.' He started tapping in its details.

'Lives underground,' said Tom. 'Eats fruit and has huge eyes!'

Jamie studied the screen. 'I can't find anything,' he said at last. 'I've put in all the details . . . but there's no match.'

Tom gasped. 'Do you think that means . . . '

'We've found a new dinosaur!' Jamie shouted.

ROOAAR!

The boys swung round. The allosaurus was still peering over the edge of the canyon.

'Oh no!' exclaimed Jamie. 'It's still waiting for a Tom and Jamie pudding.'

'Maybe if we creep across the plains,' whispered Tom, 'it might not spot us.'

They hurried across towards the jungle as quickly and quietly as they could.

Jamie looked back to see the
allosaurus sniffing around where they
had come out of the cavern.
Then it turned to face them.

'I just hope the wind doesn't
change,' Jamie said.

ROOAAR!

The allosaurus waved its head angrily and began to stomp towards them, sniffing every few steps.

'We need to mask our scent,' said Jamie. 'Then we won't smell so tasty.'

'Got an idea,' yelled Tom, veering off in another direction. 'But you're not going to like it.'

'I'll like anything better than being allosaurus pudding,' Jamie shouted back.

'Then follow me!' Tom sprinted faster. Wanna ran alongside.

As the allosaurus charged across the plains towards them, Jamie suddenly realized where Tom was heading—the piles of steaming allosaurus poo.

'Oh no!' he yelped.

'It's our only chance,' insisted Tom.

ROOAAAAR!

Jamie didn't need telling twice. Keeping his mouth and eyes tightly closed, he dived into the stinking mess.

PLUMPH!

Tom and Wanna joined him.

Jamie could feel the ground shaking with the approach of the allosaur, and then things went still.

Jamie forced his head out of the sticky poo and opened his eyes. The allie was towering over them. Tom and Wanna popped up beside him. 'Keep still,' he muttered, trying not to open his mouth.

The allosaur looked about and sniffed the air uncertainly. It stamped its feet a few times. At last it lumbered off.

'Phwar!' Jamie and Tom burst out of the brown pile and shook like a couple of wet dogs, sending flecks of allie poo flying everywhere.

Wanna was covered as well, but he didn't seem to notice the dreadful smell.

'There's only one place I want to be now,' said Tom. 'In the shower!'

'Agreed,' nodded Jamie. They set off across the plains and into the thick jungle, washing themselves as much as they could at the first stream they came to.

When they reached Wanna's cave they picked him a huge pile of gingkoes and left the little dinosaur munching happily. They stepped backwards in the dino prints back into Dinosaur Cove and the moment they were in the smugglers' cave, what was left of the allosaurus poo turned to dust.

Tom laughed. 'I wish the smell would go too.'

Jamie went to pull out his torch but then remembered, 'That cave dino broke my torch. We'll have to feel our way out.'

Once out of the cave, the boys rushed back to the lighthouse and escaped into the museum office to avoid the crowd of visitors.

'While we're here, let's research our mystery dino,' Tom said, scanning the rows of dino books.

'I'll try the Build-a-Dino program,' Jamie said. He sat down at his dad's computer and typed away. 'Beak, claws, cave dweller . . . ' After entering the colour, the size of the eyes, and the noise it made, he hit the enter key.

'That's close enough,' said Tom as an image appeared on the screen. 'Is there a match?'

Jamie held his breath and then the words 'UNKNOWN DINOSAUR' flashed across the screen.

74

'Wow!' said Tom. 'We really discovered a dinosaur.'

The boys did a high five.

'Hello, boys.' Jamie's dad came in with an armful of posters and glanced at the screen. 'That's one weird dinosaur you've invented.' He put the posters down on a shelf. Then he sniffed the air. 'Phwar! Can you smell something? It's like rotten eggs!'

Jamie grinned at Tom.

'What are you going to call your new dinosaur?' Jamie's dad asked.

'Hmm,' Tom replied. 'Maybe caveosaurus . . . or screechiosaurus . . .'

'I've got it.' Jamie laughed. 'Torchbreakiosaurus!'

Wow!

UNKNOWN DINOSAUR

DINOSAUR WORLD

- - - - BOYS' ROUTE

Humongous
Waterfall

Massive Canyon

Plains

Fin Rock

Jurassic
Ocean

Misty Mountains

Thick Jungle

Gingko Cave

Discovery Hills

GLOSSARY

Allosaurus (al-oh-sor-us)—one of the largest meat-eating dinosaurs and one of the fiercest predators of its time. Its name means 'different lizard' because its backbone was shaped differently than other dinosaurs.

Cycads (si-kads)—plants with thick trunks, palm-like leaves and cones.

Gingko (gink-oh)—a tree native to China called a 'living fossil' because fossils of it have been found dating back millions of years, yet they are still around today. Also known as the stink bomb tree because of its smelly apricot-like fruit.

Jurassic—from about 150 to 200 million years ago, the Jurassic age was warm and humid, with lush jungle cover and great marine diversity. Large dinosaurs ruled on land, while the first birds took to the air.

Predator—an animal that hunts and eats other animals.

Pterosaur (ter-oh-sor)—a prehistoric flying reptile. Its wings were leathery and light and some of these 'winged lizards' had fur on their bodies and bony crests on their heads.

Therizinosaurid (ther-izzy-no-sor-id)—a relatively newly discovered dinosaur with long neck, wide body, and large, sickle-like claws. It is believed to be related to birds because of the shape of its hip bones.

Wannanosaurus (wah-nan-oh-sor-us)—a dinosaur that only ate plants and used its hard, flat skull to defend itself. Named after the place it was discovered: Wannano in China.

I may be big . . .
but I'm hard to find

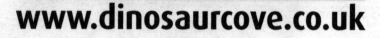